MOST PEOPLE IN OUR COMMUNITY ARE DECENT, HARDWORKING CITIZENS WHO PURSUE THEIR OWN INTERESTS LEGALLY AND WITHOUT INFRINGING ON THE RIGHTS OF OTHERS...

...BUT THERE ARE ALSO MONSTERS IN OUR COMMUNITIES... PEOPLE WHO ARE WILLING TO STEAL AND TO KILL... PEOPLE WHO DISREGARD THE RIGHTS OF OTHERS...

29

BOBO
EVANS

A
B
C
D
LET'S SEE, NOW...YOU DON'T KNOW THIS MAN AND YET WHEN YOU ASK HIM WHERE HE GOT THE CIGARETTES HE'S GOING TO TELL YOU THAT HE GOT THEM FROM A HOLDUP IN WHICH HE WAS INVOLVED AND IN WHICH A MAN WAS KILLED?
"IF HE WANTS TO RUN HIS MOUTH..."
"...THAT'S HIS BUSINESS."

43

54

THAT WAS WHAT I WAS THINKING ABOUT, WHAT WAS IN MY HEART AND WHAT THAT MADE ME.

I'M JUST NOT A BAD PERSON.

I KNOW THAT IN MY HEART I AM **NOT** A BAD PERSON.

"I'VE **NEVER** SEEN MY FATHER CRY BEFORE. HE WASN'T CRYING LIKE I THOUGHT A MAN WOULD CRY. EVERYTHING WAS JUST POURING OUT OF HIM, AND I HATED TO SEE HIS FACE."

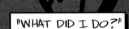

"WHAT DID I DO?"

"WHAT DID I DO?"

"I'M GOING TO HAVE TO DO SOME EDITING."
"I CAN'T STOMACH THIS PART OF THE TRIAL."
"IT'S TOO REAL. I'LL START WITH THIS SECTION."

IT WAS A REGISTERED GUN. THAT PERMIT WAS IN EFFECT SINCE 1999.

SO THERE WAS NOTHING UNUSUAL OR ILLEGAL ABOUT THE GUN BEING IN THE DRUGSTORE? IS THAT CORRECT, MR. FORBES?

I ARRIVED AT THE SCENE AT 5:15. THE BODY OF THE VICTIM WAS LYING HALFWAY... HIS LEGS WERE HALF STICKING OUT FROM BEHIND THE COUNTER.

I DIDN'T KNOW AT THE TIME IF IT WAS THE GUN THAT KILLED THE VICTIM OR NOT.

WE CHALKED THE BODY SO WE COULD TURN IT OVER AND SEE IF THERE WAS ANY POSSIBLE EVIDENCE BENEATH THE VICTIM.

THE GUYS AT THE MEDICAL EXAMINER'S OFFICE WANTED TO MOVE THE BODY.

IT WAS TIME FOR THEIR SHIFT TO END...AND I ALLOWED IT.

THE AUTOPSY I CONDUCTED REVEALED A COMBINATION OF TRAUMA TO THE INTERNAL ORGANS... AS WELL AS BY THE LUNGS FILLING WITH BLOOD.

YOU MEAN HE LITERALLY DROWNED IN HIS OWN BLOOD?

"AS MUCH AS I WANT TO I CAN'T CUT THIS OUT."

" I FINALLY UNDERSTAND WHY THERE ARE SO MANY FIGHTS."

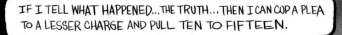

IF I TELL WHAT HAPPENED...THE TRUTH...THEN I CAN COP A PLEA TO A LESSER CHARGE AND PULL TEN TO FIFTEEN.

"ARE YOU TELLING THE TRUTH TODAY?"

YEAH.

"NOTHING FURTHER. YOUR WITNESS, MR. BRIGGS."

"AND YOU DIDN'T SPEAK TO HIM AFTER THE STICKUP OR SPLIT ANY MONEY WITH HIM?"
"I TOLD YOU WE DECIDED TO LAY LOW. WE WOULD HAVE GIVEN HIM HIS CUT LATER WHEN THINGS COOLED DOWN."
"DID THAT TIME EVER COME?"
"I DON'T KNOW WHAT KING DID."
"BUT AS FAR AS YOU KNOW... THERE WAS NO MONEY GIVEN TO MR. HARMON."
"I DON'T KNOW WHAT KING DONE."
"NOTHING FURTHER."
"THE PEOPLE REST."

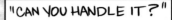

124

"ONE LAST QUESTION. WERE YOU IN ANY WAY INVOLVED WITH THE CRIME THAT WE ARE DISCUSSING HERE? TO MAKE IT CLEAR: WERE YOU... IN ANY WAY... INVOLVED WITH THE HOLDUP AND MURDER THAT OCCURRED ON THE 22ND OF DECEMBER?"
NO. I WAS NOT.
"NOTHING FURTHER. MS. PETROCELLI."

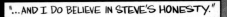
"...AND I DO BELIEVE IN STEVE'S HONESTY."

"AS A MATTER OF FACT, YOU LIKE HIM QUITE A BIT, DON'T YOU?"

"YES, I DO."

"NOTHING FURTHER."

"HARMON RESTS."

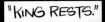
"KING RESTS."

"...I BELIEVE THAT JUSTICE DEMANDS THAT YOU REJECT THE TESTIMONY OF THESE MEN... CONSIGNING THEIR STORIES TO THE AREA OF DEEP DOUBT.... I BELIEVE THAT JUSTICE DEMANDS THAT YOU RETURN A VERDICT OF **NOT GUILTY.**"

"...IT'S UP TO YOU...THE JURY...TO FIND **GUILT** WHERE THERE IS **GUILT.** IT IS ALSO UP TO YOU TO ACQUIT WHEN GUILT HAS NOT BEEN PROVEN. THERE IS NO QUESTION IN MY MIND THAT IN THIS CASE...AS REGARDS **STEVE HARMON**... GUILT HAS NOT BEEN PROVEN. I AM ASKING YOU...ON BEHALF OF **STEVE HARMON**...AND IN THE NAME OF **JUSTICE**...TO CLOSELY CONSIDER ALL OF THE EVIDENCE THAT YOU HAVE HEARD DURING THIS LAST WEEK. IF YOU DO...I'M SURE YOU'LL RETURN A VERDICT OF **NOT GUILTY**...AND THAT WILL BE THE **RIGHT** THING TO DO...."

"... MR. HARMON WAS INVOLVED. HE MADE A MORAL DECISION TO PARTICIPATE IN THIS 'GETOVER.' HE WANTED TO 'GET PAID' LIKE EVERYBODY ELSE. HE IS AS GUILTY AS EVERYBODY ELSE...NO MATTER HOW MANY MORAL HAIRS HE CAN SPLIT. HIS PARTICIPATION MADE THE CRIME EASIER. HIS WILLINGNESS TO CHECK OUT THE STORE... NO MATTER HOW POORLY HE DID IT...WAS ONE OF THOSE CAUSATIVE FACTORS THAT RESULTED IN THE DEATH OF **MR. NESBITT.** NONE OF US CAN BRING BACK **MR. NESBITT.** NONE OF US CAN RESTORE HIM TO HIS FAMILY... BUT THE 12 OF YOU...YOU 12 CITIZENS OF OUR STATE...OF OUR CITY...CAN BRING A MEASURE OF JUSTICE TO HIS KILLERS, AND THAT'S ALL I ASK OF YOU...TO REACH INTO YOUR HEARTS AND MINDS AND BRING FORTH A MEASURE OF **JUSTICE**...."

"LAST NIGHT I WAS AFRAID TO GO TO SLEEP. IT WAS AS IF CLOSING MY EYES WAS GOING TO CAUSE ME TO DIE."

"THERE IS NOTHING MORE FOR ME TO DO."

"THERE ARE NO MORE ARGUMENTS TO MAKE. NOW I UNDERSTAND WHY SO MANY OF THE GUYS WHO HAVE BEEN THROUGH IT BEFORE...WHO HAVE BEEN AWAY TO PRISON...KEEP TALKING ABOUT APPEALS."

"THEY WANT TO CONTINUE THE ARGUMENT...AND THE SYSTEM HAS SAID THAT IT IS OVER."

"MY CASE FILLS ME. WHEN I LEFT THE COURTROOM AFTER THE JUDGE'S INSTRUCTIONS, I SAW MAMA CLINGING TO MY FATHER'S ARM. THERE WAS A LOOK OF DESPERATION ON HER FACE. FOR A MOMENT I FELT SORRY FOR HER...BUT I DON'T ANYMORE."

"THE ONLY THING I CAN THINK OF IS MY CASE. I LISTEN TO GUYS TALKING ABOUT APPEALS AND I AM ALREADY PLANNING MINE."

"EVERY WORD THAT HAS BEEN SAID IN COURT IS BURNED INTO MY BRAIN. 'STEVE HARMON MADE A MORAL DECISION,' MS. PETROCELLI SAID. I THINK ABOUT DECEMBER OF LAST YEAR. WHAT WAS THE DECISION I MADE? TO WALK DOWN THE STREETS? TO GET UP IN THE MORNING? TO TALK TO KING? WHAT DECISIONS DID I MAKE? WHAT DECISIONS DIDN'T I MAKE? BUT I DON'T WANT TO THINK ABOUT DECISIONS...JUST MY CASE."

"...JUST MY CASE."

"NOTHING IS REAL AROUND ME EXCEPT THE PANIC. THE PANIC AND THE MOVIES THAT DANCE THROUGH MY MIND. I KEEP EDITING THE MOVIES...MAKING THE SCENE RIGHT...SHARPENING THE DIALOGUE. A 'GETOVER'? I DON'T DO 'GETOVERS.'"

"IN THE MOVIE IN MY MIND, MY CHIN IS TILTED SLIGHTLY UPWARD. I KNOW WHAT RIGHT IS...WHAT TRUTH IS. I HAVE NO DOUBTS...MORAL OR OTHERWISE."

"I PUT STRINGS IN THE BACKGROUND... CELLOS...VIOLAS...."

This is the true story of Steve Harmon. **This is the story of *his life and of his trial.***

It was not an episode that he expected. It was not the life or activity that he thought would fill every bit of his soul or change what life meant to him.

He has transcribed the images and conversations as he remembers them

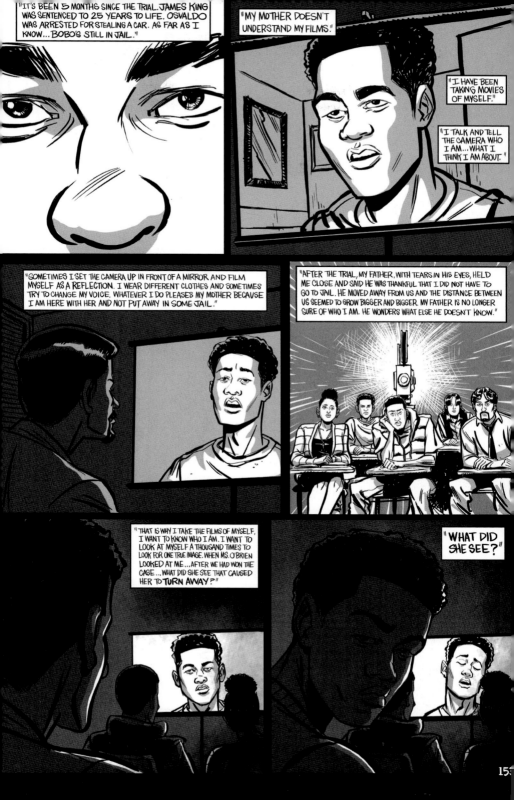

155